LiFE iS UNFAiR

LiFE iS UNFAIR

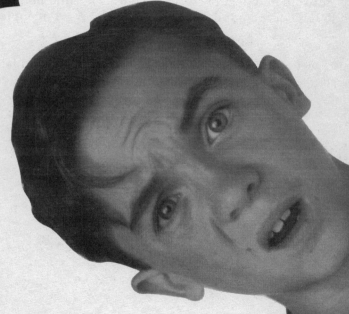

ADAPTED BY TOM MASON & DAN DANKO

SCHOLASTIC INC.
New York   Toronto   London   Auckland   Sydney
Mexico City   New Delhi   Hong Kong

TM & © 2000 Twentieth Century Fox Film Corporation, Regency Entertainment (USA), Inc., and Monarchy Enterprises B.V. Published by Scholastic Inc. All Rights Reserved.

ISBN 0-439-22840-9

12 11 10 9 8 7 6 5 4 3 2 1   0 1 2 3 4 5 6/0
Printed in the U.S.A.
First Scholastic printing, November 2000

LiFE iS UNFAiR

Book Me!

Hi, it's me. Malcolm. Now I know what you're thinking. A book called Malcolm in the Middle? Hey, if you're anything like me, you're probably scratching your head and wondering, "Why'd I pick this up?", "Where are the pictures?" and "What's on TV?"

Of course, if you're anything like my little brother Dewey, you'd just be scratching, then trying to lick the glue off the binding. But don't go there. Trust me.

If you're like my brother Reese, you'd have already chucked this across the bookstore and nailed someone in the head. You'd be giggling and pointing.

Then again, if you were like my even older brother Francis, you'd find a way to pretend you were reading it while actually reading something you aren't supposed to. Francis is the coolest.

Okay, enough about us. Now let's talk about you and what you're doing with a book in your hands. Maybe your dad said, "Kiddo, reading is fundamental." That's something my dad would say, just before he picked up the TV remote.

Or maybe your mom yelled, "Turn off the TV! Get off the Internet! Go read a book!" Oh, wait . . . that's something my mom would say.

Me? I'm just the kid stuck in the middle. Trying to be normal and not always making it. You can relate to that, right? So go ahead, my friend, turn this page and start reading. I dare you.

But pay for the book first. This isn't a library.

CHAPTER ONE

"**M**alcolm, Reese, Dewey! *Now!*"

Uh-oh, morning. That's my mom's first call to breakfast. I had at least three more minutes before I had to get out of bed. Unless . . .

Too late.

Dewey rolled over and did something that rippled our covers like waves on a cotton ocean. I don't even *want* to know what it was.

I sat on the edge of the bed and rubbed the sleep from my eyes. Reese was still asleep. His left nostril squeaked like his head was full of mice.

Dewey sprawled across our shared double bed. His bare feet kicked against my back. That's right. Kicked.

The alarm clock radio clicked on. Reese sat up and smacked me with his pillow. "Hit the snooze button, moron," he said without opening his eyes, and plopped back down to resume his nasal symphony. Dewey rolled over, and the sheets rippled again.

"Malcolm! Reese! Dewey! Get in here this instant! I'm not gonna call you again!" Mom's voice rattled the windows. I slid out of bed and shuffled to the bathroom. The best thing about childhood is that at some point, it stops.

Minutes later, the three of us trudged into the kitchen like prisoners on a forced march. I heard the whir of electric clippers. My mom, the "Mad Barber of Linoleum," was at it again.

With her brown hair piled on her head, my mom has that frazzled look of anyone with four kids like me and my brothers. But the first thing you'll notice about my mom is her eyes. They're big and brown and are like these X-ray laser beams that can see through anything. I swear, she can see through walls easier than she can see through Francis's lies.

Clipping Dad's hairy body was a monthly ritual. He looked like a werewolf if it wasn't done regularly. It's totally freaky watching the hair buzz off him. When it's all over, he's pink and smooth as a baby's bottom; if a baby's bottom had stubbly black hair, of course.

"Hold still, dear," Mom said. "I don't want to miss a spot." She ran the clippers up and down my hairy dad, who stood naked in the kitchen reading his morning paper.

Do I need to see this at breakfast? I don't think so.

"There's only two toaster waffles," Mom said without looking up. "So one of you has to have cereal."

"It's not gonna be me," Reese exclaimed. All three of us bolted for the refrigerator. I yanked open the door. Reese dove into the freezer hands-first and grabbed the frost-coated waffle box, squeezing it tight. Two frozen waffles popped into the air. Reese snagged one, and I got the other.

"Hey! No fair," Dewey whined. "You cheated! Give it! C'mon!"

"Grow taller, shrimp," Reese replied. He jerked down the toaster arm in a smooth move that ended with a punch to Dewey's shoulder.

"Ow," Dewey cried.

If everyone did evolve from lower life-forms, Reese is still a work in progress. He's a little taller than me so he gets more wind-up in his punch. He's got beady little eyes, and when he laughs, his head bobs around like those stupid big-headed dolls you see in the back of old cars.

"Enjoy your bran flakes, doofus," Reese added. He pulled the waffle out and plopped it on a plate. Dewey grabbed the cereal box and held it tight — he wasn't taking a chance with *that* one.

Dad put down the paper and looked at us. "Hey, have some consideration," he said. "There are people in this house trying to forget they have kids."

"Sorry, Dad," we said in unison, and sat at the table. Dewey unhappily dragged the box of cereal behind him.

"Ouch." Dad jerked forward. "Honey!"

"Sorry," Mom said as she rubbed her fingers across the clipper blade. "These are dull already. Honestly, Hal, you're like a monkey." She spun Dad around so his back faced the kitchen table. Like *that's* what I want to look at while I'm eating a half-frozen waffle with no syrup?

"Take a good look, boys," Mom said. "This is your future. You've got maybe five more years of being cute, then you start sprouting hair like a bunch of Chia Pets. And it never ends. It's an itchy, overfertilized lawn that bursts through your shirt."

So my dad's an ape. But so was King Kong and he did pretty good for himself until he fell in love. I guess you could say the same about my dad? He's goofy-looking like some dads, except for those old man reading glasses he wears at the end of his nose. My dad's never seen the inside of a gym, but he's still in pretty good shape. Being married to my mom is all the exercise any man would need.

"Arms up," Mom instructed. Dad raised the paper over his head and tried to keep reading.

"That Dagwood never learns," he chuckled.

Mom continued buzzing Dad. Think it can't get worse? One minute later, she drops this total bomb on me. "Oh, Malcolm," she starts off sweetly. "You have to come right home from school today. I made a play date for you with Steve Kenarban, and you have to take a bath."

"What? Mom! *No!*" I was horrified. Taking a bath was bad enough, but a *play* date? What's she trying to do? Humiliate me to death?

Reese hit the taunt buttons. "Malcolm has a play date!"

"Shut up, Reese. Mom, I —"

"With 'Stevie the Wheelie' Kenarban. Oh, man!" Reese doubled over with laughter and shoveled in a huge bite of waffle.

"Shut up! Mom, make Reese shut up!" I whined my best whine.

Reese choked on his breakfast — and kept laughing. Mom walked over and Heimliched him. A piece of waffle shot through the air. It landed in Dewey's cereal bowl.

"Cheaters never win," Dewey said, crunching the lone waffle piece.

My dad sighed. "So, Malcolm, why is playing a problem for you?"

Can you believe I actually have to *explain* this?

"First off, you only have 'play dates' when you're, like, five. Second off, I don't even *know* Stevie."

Mom was confused. "I saw his mom at the grocery store. She said you boys ate lunch together."

"*One time!*" I exclaimed. "He rolled his wheelchair over to me, and I couldn't say go away. He's not even in my class. He's in the Krelboyne class. In the *trailer.*" I paused. "Next to tetherball."

Did I need to explain everything to her?

She wagged the clippers in front of my face. Bad sign. And then she started: "You listen to me, young man. That one lunch obviously meant a lot to Stevie. He's a human being, with human feelings. Now you're gonna be friends with that crippled boy and you're gonna like it. Understood?"

"Yes, ma'am." I sighed. "Understood." If I shut up now, maybe I wouldn't get *the lecture*.

"You kids don't know how lucky you are," she started.

I winced. Incoming: the lecture.

"You just take your legs for granted," she continued, "like nothing could ever happen to them. Well, let me tell you, that is just wishful thinking. There's meningitis, car accidents . . . I could be giving you a spanking and accidentally snap your spinal cord! Every day is a lottery, and first prize is you don't have to push yourself around town on a skateboard with your hands. Think about *that*."

Reese and I went mute. We pretended to think about that very thing.

Dewey piped up. "I don't take my legs for granted, Mom."

"I know, honey," mom replied. "You're a good boy. Now quit playing with yourself and get ready for school."

CHAPTER TWO

Every morning at 8:15, the routine begins. Dads kiss Moms good-bye and leave for work so fast it's like the "Get Away from Your Kids Auto Race."

Today was no different. Dad left nothing behind but exhaust fumes as Reese, Dewey, and I stood on the porch. Mom held out three worn lunch bags. Recycling is one thing, but these looked like we had reused them since 1990. And now that I think about it? We had.

"I ran out of ham," she announced. "So one of these has egg salad. Eat it before noon, or it'll start to smell like Aunt Jackie's bathroom."

Which, as a matter of too-much-information, is an improvement over Aunt Jackie herself.

"And don't ditch your little brother today," Mom called out after us. "I don't want him kidnapped."

Dewey is my little baby of a brother. As a first-grader, he has one of those innocent faces like you see on a doll at Toys "R" Us. He also has what I call the "frying pan" look. He always looks clueless, like he just got hit over the head with a frying pan.

We turned down the sidewalk as Mrs. Gleusteen hammered a FOR SALE sign into her front yard. She whacked the post four times, then shot an angry look toward my house. There was a FOR SALE sign in Mr. Stratton's yard as well. Neighbors are such copycats.

"It's your turn to walk with him," Reese informed me, pointing to Dewey.

"Is not. I walked him yesterday," I replied. "*And* the day before."

"*I* walked him when he wet his pants," Reese bragged.

"He did," Dewey said, smiling.

I lost. Pee pants wins over a double walk every time.

Reese took off down the street. "See you in school. But don't speak to me. Are we clear on that?"

Reese disappeared around the corner. Dewey held out his hand. "Mom said to hold hands."

I pushed it away. "She did *not* say to hold hands. I'm not holding hands, Dewey."

"Come on, hold hands. Please?" Dewey waved his paw in front of me.

"No!" I said emphatically. "You're in the *first grade* now. You're too big for that. Now come on."

Dewey shuffled along and gave the sidewalk his most tragic expression. I *hate* when he does that.

"Look, I'm walking right next to you," I pointed out. "That's like holding hands without the hands."

Dewey stopped.

"What? You're not wet again, are you?"

Dewey shook his head. Whew! When he looked up

at me, his eyes widened like a sick deer. He blinked several times and stared at me for what seemed like forever — or the time it takes to stand in line at Blockbuster.

"Aargh!" I yelled. I grabbed Dewey's hand and stomped down the street, dragging him along. Which finally satisfied the little dork. "This is why everyone teases you!"

At the next block, this redheaded kid named Richard skipped up with his Britney Spears lunch box. "Hey, Malcolm," he said in his high-pitched voice. "Stuck with Dewey again?"

Richard is the only kid on the block allowed to play with us, probably because we hadn't trashed his house yet. He always spoke in the form of a question, like walking *Jeopardy*.

Richard goes, "So my mom? She says your brother? Got thrown in jail? And that's why we don't see him anymore?"

"It's not jail, dipwad," I defended. "Francis is at the prestigious Marlin Academy. It's *only* one of the best private schools in the country. He gets free haircuts and his own uniform."

Francis is my sixteen-year-old brother. He's not a bad kid. He just put the "D" in delinquent *and* too many D's on his report card. And he has bad luck with things like the police, ex-girlfriends, and car fires. Something about not knowing right from wrong, as well as right from left. At least that's what the social worker said.

11

We rounded the corner — and stopped dead. About half a block ahead was trouble: two-legged, two-fisted trouble.

"Spath!" Richard gulped.

If you lined up all the mean kids since the dawn of time and asked the meanest one to step forward, they'd all bow to Dave Spath. "They" said he had a million dollars in extorted lunch money in some secret Swiss bank account. I don't know who "they" are, but "they" know plenty about Spath's finances.

Spath's two cronies — a baboon in a sweatshirt and a freckled ape in a denim jacket — watched their knucklehead leader dangle a smaller kid by his shirt collar.

"Welcome to Dave Spath's Morning Punch-a-Thon," Spath said to the smaller kid. "Here's the way it works. You can beg for mercy on your belly, lick the bottom of my shoes, or take a beating. You must pick at least two, but if you take three, you get a pass for the next two weeks. That's really your best value."

Spath's cronies chuckled.

"You have ten seconds to choose correctly," Spath threatened, "or *I'll* choose for you." He turned to one of his monkeys. "Start the clock."

"Ten ... nine ... eight ... uh." The baboon stopped — unsure.

"Seven," Spath offered.

"Seven, right," the baboon continued. "Six ..."

My thinking? I didn't want to be the next contestant. "We'll go around the block." I grabbed Dewey's arm. "What do you do if he catches you?" I quizzed Dewey.

"Roll into a ball."

"And if he starts kicking you?"

"Stay in a ball," Dewey answered proudly.

"Good. Now come on." I shoved Richard in front of us. "And try to stay upwind." We crossed the street, our eyes never moving from Spath.

The small boy in Spath's grip winced and closed his eyes. Spath cocked his fist, then stopped in mid-punch. Spath's eyes narrowed. He sniffed the air.

Uh-oh.

"Wait," Spath said.

"What is it, boss?" the freckled ape asked. Spath shushed him and sniffed again. His face twisted and turned as though solving a complex math problem, which for Spath is pretty much *any* math problem. But our scent was gone. The trail had grown cold.

"Never mind," Spath said. He cocked his fist again.

CHAPTER THREE

If Reese had art class, there'd be so much paint splattered on the walls you'd think the room had been visited by alien cannibals. My art class was much quieter. With pencils, charcoal sticks, paints, and brushes, I got to draw tennis shoes, bowls of fruit, and curtains. Hey, it beats history.

I dipped my brush into a small canister of tempera paint and splashed it on my canvas. I stood back and admired my handiwork.

"Okay, class," Miss Hogan, my art teacher, said. "Let's wrap up these projects and move on." Her voice was thin and nervous. She was wound just a little too tight, like a cheap Swiss watch without all the Swiss parts.

"Those of you finished with your paintings may bring them up here and start on your charcoal still lifes," she explained. "You may take two pieces of fruit only, and please be careful with them. I bought them with my own money."

Miss Hogan stared at the oranges, apples, grapes, pears, and limes that sat on her desk like so much Matisse.

"My *own* money," she repeated bitterly.

Spath sat at a table behind me. He worked on his own painting like his brush was a jackhammer. It was black paint splattered on a blue background. He called it One Thousand Black Eyes.

Julie Houlerman sat next to me. She's the only girl in class who talks to me without being spoken to first. I like that. She took a break from her painting — a row of daisies with smiley faces surrounded by petals — and leaned over.

"God, Malcolm." She was totally impressed. "That's so good."

The other kids around me leaned over to check it out. They nodded in agreement.

"It's Mars," I pointed out. "Those're my brothers, hanging over the acid pit. See? The flames are just starting to burn their feet. I call it Happiness."

"It's really cool," Julie said. She smiled at me. I like Julie and she likes me. Well, I think she does. Sort of. Maybe. Girls are tricky that way. If only she'd punch me in the arm, then I'd know for sure.

I carried my painting to Miss Hogan. "Malcolm, this is wonderful," she enthused. "The perspective is good, the composition is clean, it even shows signs of actual technique. I have to say, this is the high point of my day." She turned from the painting and added, "How's that for sad?"

"Um," I stumbled for the right word. "Thanks."

I grabbed some fruit and escaped to my desk. I plopped into the seat. Instantly, I knew something was wrong. Butts shouldn't make squishy sounds. I looked down. Red paint oozed from under my pants. Doom.

From behind me, Spath snickered. I'd been Spathed.

Kill me now.

"You okay?" Julie asked. Oh, now it was worse. *Much* worse.

"Yeah. Yeah. I'm fine. Really," I fibbed.

Before I could think of anything else to say, one of those older students who thinks it's cool to spend his free time doing volunteer work at the office? He came in the classroom and handed Miss Hogan a note.

"Malcolm?" Miss Hogan said as she looked up from the slip of paper.

"Yes?" I replied nervously.

"You're wanted in the office." The words echoed from Miss Hogan's mouth like she was speaking from inside a cave.

"Okay." I didn't move. I mean, would you? The minute I stood up, everyone would see my red butt. Why couldn't I have a superpower? Something like invisibility, or time travel, or the power of self-cleaning pants.

"I think they mean right now." Miss Hogan was emphatic. The little vein in her forehead pulsed.

"Okay." I remained seated, trying to look bored. Where is a fire drill or nuclear war when you really need one?

Julie touched my shoulder. I lurched in my seat, and my butt squished again.

"Get up, Malcolm," Miss Hogan demanded. I sighed and looked at Julie, then shot a quick look back at Spath.

Spath smiled. I knew that smile. I hated that smile. I gritted my teeth and stood up. The classroom erupted in laughter as I ran out and down the hall, a bright red blob of paint covering my butt.

Julie was never going to punch my arm now.

"I Didn't Do It!"

Yeah. I've been called to the office. I know what you're thinking. But I didn't do it. Honest!

How'd that sound? I learned it from Francis. He said there are three phrases that will help any kid get through these turbulent adolescent years. The first one is: "I didn't do it." Immediately take the defensive. If you can say it first, it puts all the attention on someone else. Works like a charm. It's my favorite.

The second is: "Well, don't look at me." This is great for a denial that doesn't really deny anything or if someone's looking for you to take out the trash or wants to know who messed up the bathroom. If you can say it casually enough and keep walking, you have a chance.

The last one is: "Nothin'," which is all-purpose. It works for everything from when your mom asks "What's going on here?" to when your dad says "What'd you learn in school today, Malcolm?"

Usually, I know when I've done something wrong. I walked as slowly as I could, searching my whole brain and came up blank. Maybe wearing red paint is against school rules and I'll be sent home early.

Well, it could happen.

CHAPTER FOUR

wanted to race out the school door and head for home, but the office was closer and there'd be fewer people laughing at me. So my red butt and I went to the office. Not really the principal's office, but one of the offices in the office. I knocked on the door. A squeaky little voice told me to enter.

I stood in front of the squeaky voice that belonged to a squeaky woman sitting behind a desk. She looked like one of those people who sold home-made flowers and macramé plant holders at the local craft fair. "Hi, I'm Caroline Miller," she said as she stood up. "Are you Malcolm?"

"Yes," I replied, and just in case added, "And I didn't do it." An early denial wouldn't hurt.

"Oh. Oh. Good. Glad to hear it," she said. "Please sit down. You're not in any trouble, Malcolm."

That's good.

I gently squished into the chair. That's bad.

"You're here because some of your teachers think you . . . that you might be . . . that you have . . ."

Ms. Miller looks like one of those women who carries an old knapsack instead of a purse. Her reddish-brown hair hangs from her head like she only remembered to brush part of it. And her high-pitched voice is probably just high enough to annoy dogs. I know it was annoying me.

"I didn't do it!" Repetition never hurt.

"Look, Malcolm," Ms. Miller said, "I just want to play some games with you — puzzles, brainteasers, things like that, okay?"

"Why?" My butt's painted red and she wants to play some stupid games? Francis would know what to do. He'd fake a heart attack or double over in pain from pretend ulcers. I grabbed my side. How do you fake an appendicitis?

"Boy, you are a suspicious little dickens, aren't you?" she said. "Now come on, do this for me. I know you like puzzles."

Ms. Miller held up a large cartoon drawing that looked like one of those dopey pictures from the Sunday comics. In it, a man was driving his car toward a sunset.

"Look at this for sixty seconds," Ms. Miller explained in a soothing voice. "Then I want you to tell me everything that's wrong with it. Go!"

Like I have time for this! What if the paint's dry and I'm stuck to the seat? "The man only has four fingers," I finally said.

"Riiiight," she said, carefully drawing out the word until it had four syllables. "But I want you to take your time and *really* look —"

I pushed it away and glared at her. The red paint had finally soaked through to my skin. I needed to get out. Now. Not just out of the room but out of these pants. How idiotic is it that I had to play her little game first?

"Okay." I'll speed through this at 100 mph. *"The car's shadow is going the wrong way, the steering wheel's on the wrong side, there's no brake pedal, the words in the mirror should be backward, the guy's watch wouldn't say twelve o'clock if he's look-ing at a sunset, and* I HAVE RED PAINT ALL OVER MY BUTT!" I screamed.

"All over —" she started.

I unstuck myself and pointed to the back of my pants. "That's right! Red paint! On my butt! *That's* what's wrong with the picture!"

CHAPTER FiVE

Usually I do my best to avoid Stevie Kenarban at school. Not because Stevie was in a wheelchair — but because the kid is one of *them:* a Krelboyne. They're these scientific-genius-nerds who have their own *special* class. Their notebooks are arranged by color and size and, get this, they call their shirt pockets "writing implement containment centers." No one cool ever talked to a Krelboyne . . . unless you're a band geek, and that's something else entirely.

But this afternoon, a freshly bathed me was not only at Stevie's house, I was sitting right across from him, eating a cookie. It was torture. Talking seemed inevitable.

Stevie's in a wheelchair because of some disease I can't even begin to pronounce or spell. He's got really short black hair and wears lots of plaid J. Crew-type clothes that make him look like he lost a bet or something.

Stevie's extra-thick glasses make him look like an owl. He needs to breathe between words, so conversation moves at the speed of snails taking a nap.

I sat and chewed, staring blankly at the owl. "So what can you do?" I asked. Oops. "I mean, what do you *want* to do?"

Stevie pointed to his computer. "I could...show you...how to...program...in BASIC," he wheezed.

"No, seriously."

"I...could...show...you...my...project... for...the ...Krelboyne...Academic...Circus." His sentence lasted longer than a dental visit. "It's... pretty...cool."

"Um, maybe later." Like after aliens land and melt the earth into goo.

"I...know...a...joke," Stevie said. "A... guy...goes ...into...a...bar...and...he... has...a..." He pointed to his head. "A frog..."

I jumped in. "Frog on his head?"

"On . . . his . . . head . . . and . . . the . . . bartender...oh, wait...I...screwed...it...up. A...*frog*...walks...into...a...bar...and..."

This was hopeless, like watching a turtle stuck on its back. One thing would save me.

"You wanna watch TV? We could still catch a few cartoons."

"Can't," Stevie shook his head. "Not...allowed."

"*What?* You mean ever?" What kind of life is that? Not only is television a baby-sitter, it's a *great* baby-sitter, and a friend who is never too busy to play.

"Mom...says...TV...makes...you...stupid."

"No way," I defended. "TV makes you normal. It

helps you fit in and it explains everything to you!"
What parent would deprive a kid of television? It's
a sacred right of childhood. Mr. and Mrs. Kenarban
must be monsters. "What do you do all day?
Homework?"

"Mostly . . . read . . . comics," Stevie replied.

I lit up. "You have comic books?"

Stevie wheeled over to a closet and opened the
door. Inside was treasure; white boxes filled with
hundreds of comic books, all neatly organized
chronologically in plastic liners and labeled with
folder tabs. I was awestruck. My eyes widened as I
read the tabs. All *right*!

"Whoa. You really have *Youngblood #1*?"

"First . . . printing."

I carefully removed the comic book from the box
and slipped it out of its protective liner.

"Wanna . . . read . . . it?" Stevie asked. "It's not too
bad."

"What? No way. I'd wreck it." I slid the comic back
into the liner and back in the box. "Did you read the
Savage Dragon when they split him in two?"

"Yeah . . . brilliant." Stevie smiled.

"I like how he never has to learn a lesson or anything. He just gets to pound on everyone. He's like
my brother Francis, but he's green and has a fin on
his head."

"I . . . have . . . the . . . new . . ." Stevie stammered.

"Issue?" I said helpfully. Hopefully.

Stevie pointed to his dresser, and I grabbed the new comic book, slowly turning the pages.

"Wow." The dragon had just punched a multieyed villain through several office buildings with a *kerr-rack* sound effect.

Why don't they teach *this* stuff in school?

CHAPTER SIX

The cat smacked the mouse with a broom and drove it into the kitchen floor like a furry nail. The little rodent grabbed a hammer and removed itself from the floor, shaking back to its normal shape. The mouse reached into its too-small pocket and whipped out a too-large steam iron that it flattened against the cat's face.

Some families travel well together. Others can enjoy dinner without throwing food. The one thing my family does better than anyone else? Saturday morning. And on Saturday morning, there's nothing better than breakfast with a side order of mindlessly idiotic cartoons.

Reese, Dewey, and I sprawled on the living room sofa in our underwear, attacking our breakfast. Reese spooned from a bowl of Cheerios. I wolfed down a cold Pop-Tart. Dewey munched a piece of toast from the inside out, leaving enough crumbs in his lap to make a second piece.

The phone rang. Instantly, Reese and Dewey yelled, "Not it!" I sighed and rolled over to the phone.

"Hello?"

"Young Master Malcolm," came the reply. It was Francis!

Dewey and Reese lunged for the phone. All three of us pressed against the earpiece like Siamese triplets joined at the forehead.

Francis is tall and blond and totally cool. If he weren't away at school, he'd be the best-looking surfer on any beach. And he's always smirking, like he's saying, "I know something about you that you don't think I know."

"Look," Francis said. "I only have three minutes before roll call. I wrote you guys a really long letter. Put the special prosecutor on, okay?"

In unison, we yelled, "Mom, it's Francis!"

Mom picked up the kitchen phone. We stayed on the line. "Hey, honey," she said. "How's school?"

"Couldn't be better, Mom," Francis replied. "My new roommate showed me how to kill mice with a hammer. I really think I'm starting to turn around."

"It's just until summer, honey," Mom explained.

Francis took a deep breath. "Listen, and I know I shouldn't ask, but can you send my allowance a couple of weeks early? I need some —"

"Oh, my God!" Mom interrupted. "Francis! Are you smoking?!"

"What?" Francis said, stunned.

Could Mom actually see him through the phone? How is it that Mom always knows the unknowable? There must be some kind of Secret Mom Class that gives them special superhuman powers. How else could someone *hear* smoke?

"You're smoking," she said. "I can hear you smoking."

"No, I'm not, Mom. Geez."

"Honestly," her lecture began. "After seeing what your dad and I went through to quit? Didn't *any* of that register with you? Your lungs will go black like charcoal briquettes, and when the doctors take them out, you'll have a scar that'll make your chest look like a skin zipper."

"Right. Got it," Francis said. He'd tuned her out after the first word. It's a skill you develop with time.

"I'll talk to your dad about the money," Mom resumed. "Maybe we can send part of it, okay? I have to go, I'm late for work. I'll call you later, honey. And we'll see you next weekend."

"He is soooo lucky," Reese enthused, hanging up the phone.

"I know," I agreed. "We never go anywhere, and *he* gets to be in Alabama."

"Is Alabama nice?" asked Dewey.

"Look it up," I said. "It's got Sequoia Caverns, the biggest cast-iron statue in the world ... plus it's right next to Florida."

Dewey stared blankly.

"Where *Disney World* is!" I finally said.

"I bet he goes to Disney World all the time," Dewey added with envy.

"Hey, moron," Reese interjected. "He's sixteen. He doesn't do kid stuff. He talks to girls and goes to parties and goes skiing."

"Right, genius," I said. "They do *lots* of skiing in Alabama."

"Shut up," Reese responded with his all-purpose argument ender.

I had only one response to that. "Make me."

"Cool," said Dewey. Even he knew what was going to happen next. He flopped back on the couch to watch. Reese threw a headlock on me. We crashed into the coffee table, sending Cheerios flying into the air like breakfast confetti.

"Better than cartoons," Dewey said.

While the Home Wrestling Federation continued its Saturday Morning Bout-to-Knock-My-Stupid-Brother-Out, Mom was in the laundry room. She called out, "You better not be fighting in there. Reese? Malcolm? I said you better not be —"

The doorbell rang. "Oh, for God's sake," she said, exasperated. "Reese! Malcolm! The *door!*"

Who has time to answer the door when Reese's knee is pressed against your face? After the doorbell rang again, Mom realized that she would have to get it. We rolled out of the way as she stomped past. She flung open the front door wearing a pair of pants . . . and — oh no! — a bra!

"Yes? Can I help you?" she asked of the bell ringer. A bell ringer that turned out to be the *teacher*, Ms.

Miller! What's she doing here? At my house? On a Saturday? Aren't there rules against that?

And my mom has no top on!

Ms. Miller stammered. "Uh." That was followed by "Hi. Hello. Are you . . . ? I'm, uh, Caroline Miller. From Malcolm's school. I . . . I sent you several letters and left messages on your machine."

"Okay, fine. You caught me. What do you want?" Mom demanded.

"Well, it's been three weeks," Ms. Miller explained. "You haven't responded, and it's really important, I mean, for Malcolm's sake, that the parents be as involved as . . ."

"So you're here to insult my parenting skills?" Mom crossed her arms.

"What? No, I'm sure you're a terrific parent," Ms. Miller replied as she peeked inside the house. Me and Reese rolled past the foyer, still wrestling and punching each other. Dewey followed behind, trying to kick us.

"I'm here because I think there's a real opportunity to . . . could you, you know, maybe put a blouse on?"

"It's just underwear, lady," Mom defended. "You probably got a drawer full of it yourself. And I'm sure yours are a lot more frilly than mine."

Oh, man! Mom was giving Ms. Miller a *lecture*!

"No, yours is fine . . . ," Ms. Miller said. "I just . . . um, that's not what —"

"And I'll tell you something else," Mom continued.

"I didn't 'respond' to you because it's a load of crap. There's nothing wrong with my Malcolm and you're not gonna stick him in some special-ed class."

"But —"

"Why do you people have to label everyone? Malcolm may be a little strange, and I know he never shuts up, but that doesn't make him disturbed. He's a good boy."

"No, you don't understand," Ms. Miller said. "If I could just come in for a minute, I could explain everything. Okay?"

"Reese! Malcolm! Quit fighting and get dressed! We've got company!"

CHAPTER SEVEN

Dinner with my family is always a feast — of anything that can be microwaved, fried, or delivered, that is. Our eating habits resembled a cross between the last meal of a condemned man and a pack of coyotes fighting over a one-legged kitten.

Utensils clattered. Teeth gnashed and tore through bits of meat. Throats gulped in a symphony of gastronomic noise that would get a standing ovation at Sizzler. In less time than it took to open a can of beans, it was over. And that included the can of beans.

"S'good, hon." Dad chewed and swallowed his last bite.

Reese and I grunted with similar satisfaction and got up from the table. Reese paused to shovel in one last spoonful of beans.

"Wait," Mom stopped us. "There's something we have to talk about."

"Not Aunt Helen," Dad groaned. "I thought we weren't going to mention her until *after* her biopsy."

"It's not her," Mom corrected. "It's Malcolm."

Mom had barely finished the second syllable of

my name when I shouted, "I didn't do it!" That phrase just *had* to work sometime.

In that same instant, Reese blurted out smugly, "Yes he did. I saw him!"

Ouch. Reese unleashed the only weapon that could diffuse the "I didn't do it" defense. I was desperate. It was time for the biggest gun of all. I pointed to Reese and yelled, "You did it first!"

Mom shot both of us her "look." We shut up.

"A woman from school came by today. She tested Malcolm and he has an IQ of 165."

Dad, Reese, and Dewey looked like they'd all been hit with large boards. They stared at me, then turned to Mom.

Annoyed, Mom added, "Which means he's a *genius* and he's going to attend a special class."

Special class?! There was only one thing I could say to that: "What?" I said it several times. Just in case. Repetition in times of trouble never hurts.

"Malcolm? Special?" Dad mused. "Where do you think *that* came from?"

Mom explained that my school had a special program for gifted children. I'd get advanced textbooks, special teachers, and "all kinds of good things they don't want to waste on normal kids." She smiled at me. "You start on Monday."

Reese smiled, too — evilly. "You're gonna put Malcolm in the Krelboyne class?" The word *Krelboyne* rolled out of his mouth with equal parts contempt and excitement.

"Not the Krelboynes!" I yelped. "Mom, no! I don't want to!"

"What are you talking about?" Mom said. "Of course you want to."

"I don't want to be a Krelboyne," I pleaded. "I want to stay with my own class." Being a Krelboyne would destroy my life. My normal friends would abandon me. Julie would stop talking to me. Bullies would actually seek me out. I saw myself in a plaid shirt with a white plastic pocket protector and a portable calculator. Ack!

"Mom, seriously. Krelboynes get their butts kicked," Reese said. "I know. I've kicked some myself. It's fun."

I can't believe Mom didn't understand the relationship between bullies and nerds. What was she thinking?

"Stop right there," Mom chastened. "There is nothing wrong with being smart. And there's nothing wrong with being cut from the herd. It makes you the one buffalo that isn't there when they're run off the cliff and skinned for their hides."

Buffaloes? What's she doing?

"Mom, this isn't fair. If I don't want to go, why do I have to?" I demanded.

She resorted to the all-purpose Mom Answer. "Because it isn't your choice. Your father and I have to do what's best for you."

"Is Malcolm going to Alabama like Francis?" Dewey piped up.

"Of course not," she said. "And stop playing with yourself."

"Mom, please. Don't make me go. Please!" I begged. "It isn't fair!"

"Of course it's not fair," she said. "It's the first time anyone in this family's ever been given an edge, and you're not going to waste it."

I had one last chance. Dad. He was a boy once. He'd understand. I hit him with my saddest face and even sadder voice, "Dad?"

Mom looked at Dad, too. Only she used the "look."

Dad knew he had to make a careful family-oriented decision using his Solomon-like Dad-wisdom that came from years of parent experience. If he made the wrong choice, neither Mom nor I would be speaking to him.

He picked up the iced-tea pitcher from the center of the table and looked at it. "Oh, for crying out loud! How come there's never any iced tea in this pitcher? I make a fresh batch every morning, and it's gone by the time I get home."

"I want a better family!" I cried and bolted up the stairs.

I ran into my bedroom and flopped across the bed. Mom followed and sat beside me.

"I don't want to go to special class. People think I'm weird enough already."

"I know."

I looked up at her. "I like where I am. I want to stay."

"That's because you don't understand the world yet, sweetie," she said in the Mom Voice she uses to explain why I can't get what I really want. "Life doesn't give you a lot of chances to move up, even if you deserve it. Just look at your dad and me."

She patted my head. "Malcolm, I'm proud of you. You boys are so lucky. You have so many gifts other kids don't have. And I don't just mean Stevie Kenarban, either. Look at the Parker boys across the street. They may be healthy, but honest to God, they're the ugliest little boys ever born. They look like boiled beets, don't you think?"

That was so true. The ugliest ones I've ever seen.

"And those Henderson kids, that electrocuted their dog trying to get free cable? How smart can *they* be? Just remember. Any kid who makes fun of you is a creepy little loser who'll end up working in a car wash."

That shouldn't make me feel better? It did.

"You'll be okay, sweetie," she said as she left the room. "If you don't make a big deal out of it, no one else will."

A One-Way Ticket to Nerd-Vana

Big deal? It's more than a big deal. It's a huge deal. There's going to be finger pointing, name calling, and it's all gonna be directed at me. And not just from Reese.

Special class?! That's horrible! That's worse than skipping a grade. I'm being sent to nerd-vana. Oh, sure, the combined IQs of my new classmates probably surpasses the Gross National Product of some place like Buenos Aires.

But so what?

Krelboynes are kids with Band-Aids on their glasses, pencils in their shirt pockets, one black sock, and one brown sock. They can figure out the sum of adjacent angles in a triangle but can't talk to a girl without wetting their pants, or catch a baseball with anything other than their foreheads. I'm about to enter a world of classmates with asthma, P.E. excuse notes from their parents, and strange body odors that I can't even guess the origins of.

These are people who file their homework alphabetically. And now, everybody thinks I should be in the same classroom with them. Ugh! I hope they're not contagious.

CHAPTER EIGHT

"And I just can't say enough about how proud we should all be of Malcolm getting into the gifted program here at school," Miss Hogan said in front of the class on Monday morning.

Agony! I squirmed in my seat, nervously wanting to be anywhere but there. What happened to the days when I had simpler problems? Like red paint on my butt?

I focused on my desk. I was *far* from done with it. I hadn't finished carving my name in the corner, and there was still plenty of room underneath for more gum.

"Malcolm may not look any different from the rest of us, but he is. Very different."

What's she doing? She might as well hang a sign on my back that reads KICK ME, I'M A KRELBOYNE.

She tapped her head with her index finger. "Different in his *brain*. And I'd like you all to recognize that."

My brain containment unit hit the desk with a dull thud. The embarrassment was too much. I couldn't bear to watch anymore.

Miss Hogan applauded and gestured for the other

kids to join in. They all did, halfheartedly, except for Dave Spath. He clapped enthusiastically. A clap for every day he's going to kick my butt.

I summoned up the strength to look at Julie. She waved a sad little good-bye. I buried my face in my hands. I don't know for how long — the next several minutes blurred. I don't remember leaving Miss Hogan's classroom, walking down the hall, and entering the Krelboyne classroom. When I removed my hands from my face, there I was. Special class. Sitting next to Stevie Kenarban. And the teacher, Ms. Miller, was talking.

"Today we begin a new unit on the Peloponnesian War," she said. "Then we can all start on our projects for the Academic Circus. But first, I think we should all meet our new student ... someone very special who's joining us today and every day ... Malcolm."

All the Krelboynes stared at me.

"Malcolm, would you like to say a few words?" she asked. "Malcolm?"

The Krelboynes waited for some supersmart thing to erupt from my mouth. Some devastating scientific observation? A multisyllabic word no one had heard yet? All I wanted to do was dig a hole and crawl inside. The starefest continued. I had to say something. I took a deep breath. "Uh, hi, everybody. It's great to be here." I tried for sarcasm, but it came out much too nice. Francis just *has* to teach me how to fake a heart attack.

"And it's great having you with us, Malcolm. We're going to have a fun year together." Ms. Miller turned back to her desk and picked up a textbook. The other kids kept staring at me. A goofy-looking kid with stringy hair held a magnifying glass to my face.

"I'm picking up signs of intelligent life here, Captain," the stringy-haired kid said to some imaginary space cruiser.

"Stop staring at me!" I yelled at the stringy-haired kid loud enough so everyone would hear. They slowly turned their attention to their desks and opened their textbooks in unison. They were all brain-controlled zombies. Then they turned to look at me again like someone pushed the NOW LOOK AT MALCOLM AGAIN button.

I turned to Stevie. "Why do they keep doing that?"

"You're . . . new . . ." Stevie explained. "New . . . is . . . interesting."

Oh, great, so now I'm the freakiest freak in the freak show?

A kid with Eraserhead hair and tiny eyes leaned into my face.

"Pi to fifty places. Mark-set-go," the Eraserhead challenged — then with the speed of a NASCAR racer, he rattled off the answer: "3.142857142857 —"

"Turn away," I said to the human calculator. "Or I swear to God I'll pound you."

Eraserhead shrugged and turned away.

"Just . . . chill . . . out . . . Malcolm," Stevie said.

"Don't tell me to chill out." I was agitated now. "*You* chill out. No one can live like this."

"I . . . do . . . okay," Stevie offered.

"Oh, sure, you're okay because it doesn't make any difference to you! You've *always* been a freak. But I used to be normal!" Ooops. *That* wasn't good.

The class gasped, sucking nearly all the air out of the room. Everyone had heard my outburst. Krelboynes stuck together like zebras at a watering hole. They didn't talk to one another like that. The Krelboyne classroom was a sanctuary, a haven. I had violated the "Code of the Krelboyne," and on my first day, too.

"You . . . suck." Stevie wheeled away.

Everyone glared at me, even Ms. Miller. On the big list of lousy days, this was shooting up to number one.

CHAPTER NINE

I didn't think it could get worse at lunch, but it did. And it wasn't because my sandwich smelled like Aunt Jackie's bathroom.

For the first time ever, I sat by myself. I angrily bit into the mystery contained between two pieces of Wonder bread.

Other kids actually created this "Zone of Avoidance" around me. Because I was Krelboyne, the "normals" treated me as if I had some oozing rash. And thanks to my outburst in class, the Krelboynes excluded me as well. I'm now lower than low. The king of social outcasts.

Don't believe me? Get this — every time I shifted my body, the "Zone" moved with me. Being "gifted" is like being radioactive.

I saw Stevie across the schoolyard, sitting with the Krelboynes. As he ate his pudding cup, his chair rolled slightly, like an unstable ship on a concrete sea. I had to apologize sooner or later, and it looked like sooner moved faster. I walked over to him. The "Zone" spread, giving me plenty of room.

"Stevie," I said. He squeaked his wheelchair around. "Look, I'm —"

Ouch! An empty milk carton smacked my forehead. All the kids stopped eating and laughed. I whipped around and saw Dave Spath. He laughed as he high-fived his cronies. I threw down my lunch bag. That was it.

"Hey, Spath," I challenged. "Why don't you stop being such a jerk?" Whoa! Did I say that? What was I thinking? I guess I had nothing left to lose — except maybe my life.

Everyone went silent as if a switch had clicked off. They looked at me, stunned. No one stands up to a school bully. That's like trying to stop a battleship with a piece of gum. And I was out of gum.

Spath grinned. He walked over to me and stood inches from my face. Yuck. He had tuna fish for lunch.

"What did you call me?" Spath demanded, cupping his hand to his ear.

"You heard me," I said. "Jerk. Want me to spell it for you? I don't care anymore, Spath. Okay? I just don't care. All you do is make everybody miserable, except for your little monkey-slaves, who by the way only *pretend* to like you. They hate you as much as everyone else does, and you're just too busy being mean and stupid to ever figure it out."

I wanted to run, but my legs wouldn't work. That's when it hit me. Mom was right. Legs *are* important.

"Ouch," Spath said sarcastically to his monkey-slaves. "I don't know about you, but the Krelboyne kid has really hurt my feelings." The apes and baboons laughed, a little too loud, mostly to hide the fact that I was right. They *did* hate Spath.

Stevie rolled up behind me. "Hey . . ." he said.

"It's good you two are friends," Spath cut him off. "After I'm done with you, you can share his wheelchair."

Spath brought up his fists. I have no idea why I did this, but I grabbed Stevie's pudding cup from the table and shoved it in Spath's face. He staggered back. This was my chance to get away. I turned, but Spath grabbed my shirt.

He spun me around and took a wild swing just as a tiny blob of processed chocolate slid into his eyes. Saved! By pudding! I ducked the blow and Spath lost his balance, falling forward with his fist extended.

That's when things *really* got crazy.

Because Spath's fist headed directly for Stevie. Spath tried to pull it back. Stevie tried to roll away. Too late.

Spath's fist whooshed past, barely tapping Stevie on his chin.

The kids in the crowd gasped. Spath stared at Stevie with guilty horror. Spath's crony with the sweatshirt finally broke the uncomfortable silence.

"Dude," he said. "You hit a cripple."

Even he knew: No one hits a kid in a wheelchair. They're last on the list of things to hit, just after solid brick wall, hornets' nest, and little blind girl.

Stevie caught my eye and winked. He leaned to his right and tipped over his wheelchair. It fell to the ground with an awful, sickening crash. The crowd gasped even louder.

"I think . . . my . . . jaw is . . . broken," Stevie cried out in an Oscar-worthy performance.

"Horrible!" one kid said.

"Terrible!" said another.

Others shook their heads at Spath. A fifth-grade girl burst into tears.

Spath turned to the crowd.

"No, I wasn't trying to," Spath defended. "I mean, come on, I wouldn't —"

"I'm telling," one of the kids yelled and ran off.

"Me, too," another said and joined him.

"I'm sorry! Stevie! I didn't mean to —" Spath pleaded, but it was hopeless. The kids moved in to help Stevie back into his chair, and guess whose hand was there first, pulling Stevie up?

Mine.

I sat Stevie back in his chair and we shook hands. Not only were we friends again, but I had defended a Krelboyne against the forces of evil known as the school bully. Like it or not, I was now one of them.

Oh, no. It *is* contagious.

Spath Gets His

So then the principal comes out. That was the best. Everyone was talking at once and the story got wilder and wilder.

"Spath did this!"

"Spath did that!"

"I saw it all!"

Finally, the principal sorted out the truth: Spath attacked Stevie to steal his chocolate pudding cup. Even a million "I didn't do its" couldn't get Spath out of this one. He got suspended for one day, detention for a week, and has to watch a boring *"Be Kind to Your Neighbor"* video and take a quiz on what he's learned.

And me? I'm the hero for stepping in and defending Stevie. It was beautiful.

Okay, it wasn't funny when Spath started crying.

Oh, wait. Yes it was.

Stevie and I are friends again, so

that's pretty cool. But I still have to go to special class. I'm still a Krelboyne. I just gotta figure out a way to make it okay.

CHAPTER TEN

The kid with the stringy hair wrote on the black-board with the speed of an Italian sports car. He'd been at it for almost ten minutes. His dripping sweat formed little puddles on the ground. On the blackboard was a mess of mathematical symbols, geometric shapes, and arrows. He finished with the flourish of a spastic orchestra conductor and turned to face the rest of the Krelboynes.

"And if my calculations are correct," he said, "once I construct the interstellar mallet, I should be able to split the earth into four equal parts with a simple wedge."

"That's very nice, Carlos," Ms. Miller said to the young Einstein. "Let's just hope the government will approve your grant application."

It had been like this all week. The Krelboynes were busy working on their projects for this weekend's Academic Circus, a combination talent show and parent-teacher-student picnic. Pleading my case as the "new student," I had tried my best to get out of it, but Ms. Miller ix-nayed me. She wanted me to do something that would make my parents "proud."

"Proud? Ugh! You mean my parents are going to see me?" I said.

"Of course," Ms. Miller replied. "The Academic Circus is a family event. It's a chance for parents to see what their children have learned."

A total freak show by freaks for their freaky-freak parents? The last thing I wanted to do was get up in front of my family and show off. They'd probably put me up for adoption.

While I pondered the fate that awaited me at the "Freak Show-and-Tell," the other students rehearsed their "acts." A small red-haired girl stood at the front of the class. In front of her she had a small plant, a pitcher of water, and a giant lamp. "I'll be demonstrating the process of photosynthesis," she said. She turned on the lamp and watered the plant.

"In the first part of the process, light is absorbed by chlorophyll, which splits water into hydrogen and oxygen." She stared at the plant. "Look! you can almost see the plant breathe!"

I didn't see anything but a plant, a pitcher, and a lamp so bright I was getting a sunburn. She inhaled and exhaled, imitating the process of the plant. It was not a pretty sight and about as exciting as watching paint dry.

"I see it! I *can* see it breathing!" one Krelboyne yelled. The others quickly ran over and crowded around the plant.

"There! There! It's moving!" a kid named Arthur called out.

Ms. Miller leaned over the plant. "Uh . . . Arthur . . . that's a dung beetle."

"So what . . . are you . . . working on . . . Malcolm," Stevie said as he wheeled up to my desk.

"I'm working on not going," I replied. "If I can just find some food that'll give me an allergc reaction, or maybe I could fall down and break an arm, everything would be great."

"No . . . seriously. I . . . want . . . to know . . . if . . . I have . . . to . . . get my . . . game on," Stevie wheezed.

"I'll let you know," I sighed.

As the red-haired girl finished her "display," a kid named Clyde made his way to the front of the classroom carrying a large box. From the box, he spread out a chemistry set and a large test tube. He then pulled out a battered shoe box.

"Ladies and gentlemen. Fellow Krelboynes," he began. He tapped the shoe box. "My pet snake, Cleopatra, is one of the deadliest snakes on the continent of Africa. From her venom, scientists can make the only known antidote to her fatal bite."

He snapped on a protective glove that made his hand look like he was wearing a ham. "I shall attempt to milk the venom from her poison sacs, thus helping science increase its supply of the antidote." Clyde paused. His eyes swept across the anxious Krelboyne faces. The entire class inched forward on their chairs, and Clyde shot up a single finger of warning. "Do *not* try this at home."

Clyde carefully removed the lid of the shoe box. He stopped and stared inside. And stared. And stared.

"What's wrong, Clyde?" Ms. Miller finally asked.

Clyde reached into the box and pulled out what looked like a fat, multicolored noodle. It was a dead snake. Cleopatra was no more. Clyde burst into tears.

"It's okay, Clyde. There'll be other snakes," Ms. Miller said sympathetically.

Clyde turned the box upside down and shook it. "No there won't. Her babies ran away!"

Ms. Miller squealed and jumped on her desk. The Krelboynes squealed and ran out the door.

Except for me and Stevie.

"Check . . . behind . . . the . . . trash can," Stevie said.

"This is sooo cool." I crawled on the floor looking for loose baby snakes. I hope this is part of his act!

Malcolm, The Boring Freak

The act. My act. That's all I can think of. I liked it better when school was just about grades, fire drills, lunch, and getting out early. No one ever said anything about performing. That's for dogs and movie stars.

The truth is I already know what my act is going to be. Boring. Not only will I be a freak, but I'll be a boring freak; like the kid who knows Mr. Spock's first name or who can alphabetize dinosaurs by their scientific classifications.

I hate to say it, but the other Krelboynes have these really cool visual things: charts, graphs, chemicals, colored inks, baby snakes. That's the kind of stuff that really holds an audience's attention.

And me? That's it. I've got me. Just me.

Maybe Saturday won't show up this week.

CHAPTER ELEVEN

It came. Saturday morning, that is. I was having the coolest dream. I lived in a different neighborhood with different brothers. A cute girl next door who kept whispering "Malcolm . . . Malcolm . . . Malcolm . . ."

"Malcolm . . ." Reese whispered into my ear.

I slowly opened my eyes. Gunky eyeball crust held my eyelashes together. I could barely see the blurred shape of Reese. I could also barely see the blurred shape of Reese's fist flying toward my face.

"Ow!" I yelped after Reese smacked my eye.

How fair was that?

Reese jumped off the bed. I retreated under the blankets like a turtle popping into his shell.

"That's for me having to go to your stupid Krelboyne picnic today," Reese spat as he stomped away from the bed.

"You think *I* want to go?" I protested from under the blanket. I peeked out. Reese had already moved on to Dewey.

"Quiet," Dewey squeaked. "You'll wake Francis."

"Fran" and "Cis": two syllables Reese loathed to

hear. Not that he didn't like having our older brother around, but with Francis home for the weekend, Reese moved one rung down on the sibling food chain.

Francis's timing was awful for me, too. The last thing I wanted was to look like an idiot in front of my older brother.

Reese released Dewey, careful not to wake Francis, who was wadded into a sleeping ball of blankets. This gross string of drool hung from the corner of his mouth and stuck to his pillow.

"... pretty bunnies ..." Francis mumbled.

"You're off the hook this time," Reese sneered at Dewey. "But when Francis wakes up, you'd better be invisible."

Dewey raced out of the room.

I wish *I* were invisible. There must be some way to get out of this ridiculous circus? I rolled over and buried my face in the pillow. With my face pressed into the springtime-fresh pillowcase, inspiration struck harder than Reese's fist.

Outsmarting Mom

Let me explain something about this lame circus thing. I don't think I need to tell you what an absolute waste of time any parent-teacher day is, but imagine if you also had to perform some stupid act as well.

And not just any acts. Krelboyne acts. Watching them is like watching paint dry. Only worse. At least paint smells better.

Not only do I have to waste a precious weekend day at the festival of nerds when I could be doing something important, like watching TV, but I have to perform, too! I'm gonna stand up in front of a million strangers and make a fool of myself. Then they'll know I'm a freak, too...and so will my family.

Okay, maybe it's not a million, but it might as well be. And did I get a choice in any of this? Of course not! The only choice I get is when I change my underwear and socks.

And now that I think about it, I don't have a say in that, either.

But I'm not caving yet. Just wait. I've got a plan. I'll be in front of the TV with a bag of potato chips in no time. I only need to leap over the greatest obstacle of all time.

Mom.

CHAPTER TWELVE

"Gugh!"

The sound echoed down the hallway. I knew Mom could hear it, but I added an extra one to sound like I was totally dying.

"Gu-u-ugh!"

Mom appeared at the bathroom door. Let the plan begin.

Poor me. Poor, poor me. Poor, poor, poor, bent-over-the-toilet, hugging-the-sides-of-the-bowl-face-hovering-over-the-water me. Mom cautiously peered over my shoulder. A mass of mess floated in the water inches from my nose.

"Oooooohhh . . ." I groaned. I weakly lifted my head as if to say, I am so sorry for being sick on this most important of days.

"Poor baby," Mom offered sympathetically. With a motherly hand, she brushed the hairs from my forehead.

"Yeah," I said, as if the strain of uttering the single word used more strength than I could muster. "I'm sick."

"*No*, you're *grounded* — for pouring perfectly good vegetable soup into the toilet." She picked up a cubed carrot floating in the water and thrust it before my eyes.

She flushed the toilet. On her way out, she snatched the empty soup can from the back of the top shelf near the door and tossed it in the trash. "And you owe me forty-nine cents."

I closed the lid and plopped down on the cold plastic surface. "Now I *am* going to be sick."

"It works better if the seat's up," a tiny voice whispered from the clothes hamper.

I flipped open the hamper lid. Ugh! The smell! Did something die in there?

"What are you doing?" I asked.

Dewey peered up from under a damp towel. "Being invisible."

I pushed over the hamper. Dewey rolled out, along with two weeks of stinky laundry. "Come on. Let's get breakfast."

I led Dewey to the kitchen where Reese, Francis, Mom, and Dad were chowing a meal of saturated fats. Mom plopped down sausage, bacon, and eggs on our plates.

I stared into my plate, as if the gristled bacon were going to stand up and dance and I didn't want to miss a moment.

Reese ate faster than he could swallow and washed down choking-sized food chunks with swigs of OJ. Whatta pig!

Francis happily devoured his plateful of real eggs and bacon, glad to be away from Marlin Academy for the weekend. Francis said the school mess hall served some egg substitute goop and Bac*Os.

Bac*Os? Like, what's Bac*Os?

"I don't understand why you don't want to go to this picnic, Malcolm," Mom said, scraping off extra gristle for the smiling Dewey. "It sounds like fun." She stopped for a moment and sniffed Dewey. Her nose crinkled. She removed a hamper sock stuck to his back and continued serving.

"Yeah. Sitting out on the grass, eating barbecue," Dad added dreamily, biting a sausage link in half.

"It's *Krelboynes*," I protested. "It's not going to be on the grass, because half the class is allergic," I looked up from my plate. "And don't expect any meat, either, because they voted not to serve anything that's had a mother."

"No meat?" Dad stopped chewing. "Who would ever vote for anything so *un-American*?"

"Cousin Nancy doesn't have a mother," Dewey said quietly.

"That's right," Mom replied in a slow, explanatory voice. "She has two daddies."

"Oh, man!" Reese interrupted. "Two guys as your parents? That house has gotta be a dude's paradise."

Francis and I exchanged a look of horror. I was about to speak, but stopped. Ignorance is bliss.

Dad stabbed the sausage-that-once-had-a-pig-for-a-mother with his fork. On the way from plate to mouth, he stopped and pointed the fried link at me.

Grease drops shot off the end and hit me in the cheek. "You know," Dad began, waving the sausage, "there are a lot of proven health benefits to the vegetarian lifestyle. In fact, I've been seriously considering it myself." Dad devoured the last sausage piece.

"And it'll be nice to meet the other parents," Mom said, like *that* would cheer me up. "I'll bet they're much better than those carnival freaks in Reese's class. What a horrible bunch of people."

"Amen to that," Dad added, wadding the sausage in his cheek.

"Well, it sounds like a blast to me." Francis dragged his fork across his plate to scrape up the last egg bits. He licked his fork with a satisfied grin. "Why do I have to go again?"

"Because it's a family picnic, Francis, and you are a part of this family," Mom replied.

"Oh, right. I keep forgetting that," Francis shot back sarcastically, "being forced to live a thousand miles away at a military school and all."

Mom delivered a quick sarcastic smile, which Francis returned. She grabbed the plate in front of him, stacked it on Dewey's and headed to the sink.

"Hey, I wasn't —" Dewey protested.

Mom dumped the dishes in the sink atop last night's dinner plates, yesterday's breakfast bowls, and something that may have been food at one time but was now green and stuck to the inside of a casserole dish. She pulled a flyer decorated with clowns and balloons from the refrigerator.

"I for one can't wait to see this Academic Circus you're having. I bet it's really cute," she finished, showing the flyer to me.

Oh, man. She was totally making me squirm. But why? The vegetable soup? That's it. Who knew forty-nine cents meant so much to her?

"It's not a circus," I responded. "It's a bunch of social misfits doing weird stunts to show off how smart they are."

"What's your 'weird stunt,' honey?" Mom asked.

"Me," I stammered nervously. "Just some lame thing. Nothing you want to see."

I snagged Francis's sleeve and tugged him closer.

"You've got to get me out of this," I whispered.

"Why?" Francis coolly responded. "What's the big deal?"

"It just *is*, okay!" I snapped. "I don't want to do my act."

Francis unlocked my fingers from his sleeve. "All right, relax," he nodded. "We'll hang out for fifteen minutes, establish a presence, then go over the fence. Just like Grandma's wedding."

"Go over the fence . . ." the words relaxed me like a warm bath. That's why I love Francis. He's always on my side.

And he always has a plan.

CHAPTER THIRTEEN

Have you ever been to school on a weekend? It's even worse than being there during the week. But there I was — *with* my family *and* a fleet of Krelboynes.

As we approached the Academic Circus stage, Ms. Miller jumped out from behind a large tree. "Welcome! Welcome one and all!" She giggled. "Run away with us and join the circus! The *Academic Circus!*" She was dressed as a clown, with black tights, face paint, and top hat.

"Oh, Malcolm, thank goodness," Ms. Miller confided. "I was so nervous. I had a dream that you didn't come, and then I was being chased by something big and polka-dotted that . . . never mind. You're here and that's all that matters."

No, I'm *escaping* and *that's* all that matters.

Ms. Miller spotted Dewey, stuck to the ground like he had sprouted roots. "Hello, little guy," Ms. Miller squealed and flashed a large toothy grin. "Ready to leave your family and join the circus?"

Dewey's eyes widened with fear. He spun away from Ms. Miller and clenched Dad's leg like a baby possum.

Before we reached the main picnic area, I faced the hugest obstacle yet: the Krelboynes' Welcoming Committee.

Ms. Miller in a clown outfit was bad, but the Eraserhead family in *any* outfit was worse. And there was the whole clan, high-fiving the new arrivals.

My pleading eyes locked on Francis. He motioned the STAY CALM double-hand sign. "Fifteen minutes . . . make a presence . . ."

This was more than a presence. This was the Eraserheads! These goofballs had the brains of a computer, bodies like pencils, and personalities of wet noodles.

"Oh, look at all your little friends," Mom chirped.

"They're not my friends," I hissed. "They're a bunch of geeks and losers."

"Geeks and losers who are your friends," Reese happily corrected.

Before I could launch a defense, the geeks and losers spotted me. "Malcolm's in the house!" They quacked like ducks. "Mal-*colm!* Mal-*colm!* Mal-*colm!*"

I hung my head. My heart sank into my toes. Reese elbowed past, cracking his knuckles.

"Oh, man," he said, barely able to control his giddiness, "I'm gonna kick so much Krelboyne butt today it's not even funny."

Reese watched the youngest Eraserhead perform his "Cabbage Patch Dance." Reese began to shake. His heart raced in his chest and pounded so hard, even Dad cocked his head, wondering at the muffled thumping.

Calm down, Reese said to himself in a monotone voice. *Easy now. You've got all afternoon.*

I pulled Francis away from the group. "Fifteen minutes and we're outta here, right?"

Francis glanced around. School. Balloons. Clowns. Krelboynes. "Make it ten," he whispered.

Everything was going good. Right? Francis's plan was a surefire success? Right? Nothing could stop us? Right?

Wrong.

Teenage. Cute. Female. Jody — that was her name. Francis saw her sitting with her family several tables away. I never had a chance.

"Hello," Francis said to himself.

"What?" I nervously responded.

"Nothing." Francis turned to me. "These are critical moments, young master Malcolm. It's best if we weren't seen together prior to the break. We'll tell Mom different stories, and she'll never think we planned this."

Francis took off.

"Where are you going to be?" I called to him.

"Around," Francis called out, never looking back.

I stuck with Mom and Dad. They had joined a group of Krelboyne mothers chattering around a picnic table. I had to establish an early alibi with them to distort the length of my disappearance.

"Hi," my mom greeted the other Krelboyne mothers. "I'm Lois and this is Hal. We're Malcolm's parents and —"

Dorene, the self-appointed leader, stepped forward. She had the smile of a woman pretending to be interested in being a woman who pretended to be interested. Her hair was pulled back by a tight hair band. It stretched back the skin on her face like a discount face-lift.

"That's very nice," she interrupted. "I'm Dorene and these are the girls."

"The girls" gave a meek wave and then waited silently to be cued again by Dorene.

What a bunch of sheep.

"Nice to meet you," Mom warmly responded.

"Yeah, it's really —" Dad started.

My dad *wanted* to finish his sentence, but a man has priorities. His were being rearranged by a far-off gleam that caught his eyes.

The barbecue.

"Whatever," he mumbled trancelike to "the girls" and bolted for the barbecue, his cooler tucked under his arm.

"I hope everyone likes brownies," Mom said, handing Dorene her Pyrex dish.

"Oh my, that is so thoughtful," Dorene gushed.

She took the dish from Mom and froze.

"Are . . . are those *nuts*?" Dorene asked.

"Walnuts," Mom responded.

"Oh my," Dorene gasped. "We can't have that. Some of the children are allergic to nuts."

"Gosh, I had no idea. Whose kid is allergic?" Mom asked, concerned.

Like, probably *all* of them.

"Well, no one in this class specifically, but you can never be too careful," Dorene replied. She marched a few steps to a garbage can.

"Believe me, this isn't meant to publicly humiliate you," she said, a smile cracking across her lips.

Dorene whacked the Pyrex dish inside the trash can until every trace of the walnut-infested brownies was gone.

There went my lunch.

Dorene dropped the dish into my mom's hands. "I'm sure they were delicious."

This was going to get ugly. I wanted to be far away.

I caught up with my dad on his way to the Promised Land. We approached the Krelboyne fathers who had gathered around the barbecue like cavemen surrounding a fire.

"Hiya, fellas," Dad opened.

"Name's Dave. What's your pleasure?" Dave responded while noodling the grill with tongs. "Nature dog, health patty, tofu square?"

Were we supposed to eat this crud? Green soy dogs, gray veggie burgers, and a quivering something that had *never* been alive, cooked over the burning coals.

"My God!" Dad recoiled in shock. "They . . . they don't even *sizzle*."

"Want me to brown that chick-kin leg for you?" Dave asked.

Before Dad could respond, Dave grabbed a small spritz bottle. He sprayed this brown mystery liquid onto the drumstick-molded tofu. Eat *that*? I'll starve first.

Dad slowly slid the cooler from under his arm. "Well, it looks like I got here just in time," he enthused. "Gentlemen, behold."

Like a pirate cracking the lid off a treasure chest, my dad lifted the cooler top and proudly shared the wonderful prize inside. But this was better than gold doubloons and pieces of eight. This was 100 percent USDA Choice. The fathers peeked inside Dad's magic cooler. They actually gasped in awe.

"Is that . . . meat?" Dave asked.

I'm not sure if Dave was frightened or impressed.

"Nothing but," Dad proudly replied. "Fresh from the slaughterhouse to you."

The picnic was in full swing. Dads around the barbecue, moms chatting at the picnic table, and all the kids playing. Me? I counted the minutes and reviewed escape Plan A. I never realized Francis had already moved on to Plan B. Make that Plan J.

CHAPTER FOURTEEN

As in "Jody." Francis had been wandering around for several minutes looking for Jody. He finally found her behind a classroom. I came around the corner just in time to see my rescue ship hit the iceberg and disappear below the waves.

"Hi," Francis said as if he didn't care if she answered.

"Hi," Jody responded as if she never really heard him.

"So, you here?"

"Yeah, you?"

"Yeah."

That was it. In those eight words, Francis and Jody knew all they needed to know about each other. They locked into a passionate kiss.

Trouble!

"Francis! What are you — come on, the coast is — it's been ten minutes and — we're not ditching, are we?" I groaned.

Francis shooed me away like an irritating horsefly. So much for Plan A.

I slithered away and spotted Reese hiding in the bushes. He crouched at the edge of the leafy green camouflage. Reese carefully bent back one of the branches and locked on to his targets.

"A small pack of Krelboynes has ventured out of hiding to bask in the afternoon sun," Reese quietly narrated to himself in his best Discovery Channel voice. "Their defenses down, they are easy targets for nearby predators."

Suddenly, one of the Krelboynes popped his head up and sniffed at the air. His eyes darted. He quickly moved his head about in sharp, twitching motions. A second Krelboyne popped his head up as well, then a third . . . and fourth. Without making a sound, the Krelboynes huddled closer. They sensed the danger, but it was too late. Their hesitation was fatal.

Like a cheetah, Reese erupted from the bushes. The Krelboynes bolted in tight pack formation. It was cool watching them zigzag, hoping to confuse Reese. But it was not to be. Reese was on top of them. Panic swept through the pack.

"Ack! Ack! Ack!" they all shouted and shot off in different directions.

Reese had to act quickly. He locked on the slowest — Eraserhead. Reese cornered the Krelboyne. He cracked a totally wicked grin and moved in for the kill.

"And the circle of life goes on," Reese said to Eraserhead, in some lame attempt to assure him of the naturalness of getting beat up.

But before Reese knew what was happening, a big

hand reached out and grabbed him by the shoulder. Reese spun, expecting to be confronted by Mom or Dad.

He should be so lucky.

Instead, Reese found himself looking *up* at a bigger version of Eraserhead. A bigger brother version to be exact. These Krelboynes come in all sizes? Reese's head snapped from little Eraserhead to big brother Eraserhead, stunned at their nearly identical appearance. I gotta admit, it was bizarre.

"Kafkaesque, isn't it?" Eraserhead chuckled.

"Huh?" was all Reese could manage.

"Never mind," Eraserhead said and turned to his big brother. "Kick his butt!"

Big brother smiled and Reese's eyes widened like balloons. He actually looked to *me* for help. I shrugged. In a second, Reese was gone, running for his life with big brother Eraserhead in hot pursuit.

And the circle of life goes on.

CHAPTER FIFTEEN

I slumped behind the Academic Circus stage. Francis wasn't going to save me. I awaited the executioner's call. Stevie interrupted my quiet repose on death. He rolled past carrying a tray of test tubes.

"Hey, Stevie." I sighed.

"Can't stop . . . to chat," Stevie huffed. "Gotta get . . . my chemicals . . . in the shade."

"I thought you were doing oscilloscopes," I mentioned.

"Changed to . . . catalytic . . . reactions. It's more . . . visually . . . exciting." Stevie paused, then tagged on a nervous "R . . . right?"

"What do you care?" I asked.

"I'm up . . . after you."

"So?"

Stevie rolled his eyes and sighed. "Following you . . . is like . . . following . . ." Stevie paused and searched for the right word to make me understand. "Streisand!"

Streisand? Whatever.

I peeked through the backstage curtain. The circus was well under way. Dorene's son, Dabney, a short-haired, skinny boy was onstage. He stood, bent at the waist at a perfect ninety-degree angle, before a small table and a lone microscope. Dabney's right eye was pressed against the microscope's eyepiece. He raised both hands as if he were holding back the audience.

Hold them back from sleeping, maybe.

"Wait, wait, here it comes . . . yes!" Dabney yelled and shot upright. "I have arrested the cellular mitosis!" Dabney pumped his fist in the air and took a long bow. A few Krelboynes chanted, "Whoo-whoo-whoo."

Sensing the dullness of Dabney's act, Ms. Miller bounded onto the stage. "Thank you, Dabney! That was . . . riveting!" she overenthused, threatening to explode with manufactured excitement. "Our next act needs no introduction, having been the buzz of last year's Math Fair. Presenting Flora Mayesh and Fermat's Last Theorem!"

Flora shuffled out. She fastidiously set up an easel and a large poster board with a math equation. It was so complex, it looked like a pile of spaghetti without sauce. Flora faced the audience, brushed away the single lock of brown hair that perpetually fell across her eyes, and adjusted her wire-rimmed glasses.

"Now I know what all of you are thinking. 'How does this affect the differentiation and integration for finding the maxima and minima points of curves and the areas enclosed by curves?'"

"She took the words right out of my mouth." One Krelboyne actually said that to another!

While Flora knocked 'em dead — or at least comatose — with her "act," Ms. Miller slid backstage.

"This is going well, right?" she asked me, eager for reassurance.

I couldn't lie.

"It's pretty much everything I expected."

"So you're ready, Malcolm? I mean, you're all set, right?" she asked urgently.

"Sure," was what I said. "Get me outta here," "no way," "not in a million years," was what I wanted to say.

She gave me a quick smile and scurried back to the stage.

"I'm . . . ready . . . thanks for . . . asking." Stevie hurriedly added before Ms. Miller disappeared behind the stage curtain.

CHAPTER SIXTEEN

I can't believe this. I'm waiting for my turn, totally hating every second of this stupid circus and I spot the traitor Francis. He was walking with Jody, holding hands like two lovesick kids. Accent on the sick.

"You know what's so great about our relationship?" Francis bubbled. "It feels so . . . fresh. You know what I mean?"

Jody gazed into Francis's eyes. Explosions could have erupted around her and she would have never known. "Totally," she said, mesmerized.

I watched the lovebirds stroll up to Dad and Dewey, who manned the grill with their contraband meat, taking food orders from the other dads.

"I'll have two burgers and a dog, Hal," Dave happily read from a list.

"Coming up. Dewey?"

Dewey looked around to make sure no one was watching. He reached into the cooler and pulled out the meat order.

Dad took the patties and smiled down at Dewey. "What have I told you about eating raw meat, son?"

"I'm not," Dewey protested, his cheeks packed with raw meat.

Francis and Jody wedged into the group.

"Dad," Francis proudly began, "I want you to meet someone. This is Jody."

"Hi," Dad replied, not looking up from the grill.

"It's so great to finally meet you," Jody gushed. "Francis talks about you all the time."

All the time? What? All the time for the last ten seconds?

"Oh, yeah. You, too," Dad said, his mind hamburgered.

Then Dad heard a crash and quickly covered the grill. He scanned the schoolyard for the source. But it was only a Krelboyne who had knocked over a prop onstage.

The Krelboyne was Lloyd, a milky-white kid who would be sunburned by the time he left the stage. He turned to the crowd.

"Ladies, gentlemen, and *homo sapiens* of all sizes." Lloyd's voice was so nasal, he should have spoken directly out his nose and saved the wear on his jaw. "I give you the Nixon electromagnet!"

So what do you get when you mix a Krelboyne, a Nixon electromagnet, and braces? Beats the heck outta me, but it sure screams a lot.

Lloyd flipped on the POWER switch to the Nixon electromagnet. His face immediately slammed down on the pulsing magnet, stuck by the braces.

"Hurn ih hoff! Hlease hurn ih hoff," he shouted, lips pressed against the magnet.

Ms. Miller ran to the POWER switch. On a different day I might have laughed. It's hard not to when a kid's face gets stuck to a magnet by his braces. But even the tragedy that was Lloyd-and-the-Nixon-electromagnet was nothing compared to the humiliation that awaited me on that awful stage.

"This is . . . it. You're . . . almost up," Stevie said, as if on cue.

"Stop reminding me," I groaned.

"Nervous?"

"No, I just don't want to do this." I slumped. Stevie just didn't understand.

"Don't you ever get sick of being a Krelboyne?" I asked, almost accusatory. "Of people thinking you're some kind of freak?"

Stevie shook his head. "You're in . . . Krelboyne denial. Every . . . new kid . . . goes through . . . it. You are . . . what you are," he said, putting his arm around me. "I know it . . . sounds lame, but . . . being different . . . it's not that . . . bad. Accept it."

"Not without a fight!" I retorted.

"You're harshing . . . my buzz," Stevie rolled away. "Don't let anyone . . . mess with . . . my stuff."

I slumped on the ground. And that's when I saw it. Stevie's chemicals. His test tubes.

For the first time that day I smiled.

What was that formula again?

The Wrong Hands

I know what Stevie was trying to do: Make me feel all good inside about being different. "Your weaknesses are strengths" or some crud like that. But Stevie doesn't have a choice, you know? I mean he's got that wheelchair and stuff, so he's got to accept who he is. You don't see history's great men accepting themselves, do you? Men like...like... well, I can't think of any, but I'm sure if I had the time I could think of plenty.

I was serious when I said I'm going to fight this. Let other people accept me for who I am. That's why we have families, right?

Besides, Stevie won't miss his chemicals, I'm sure of it. Right now, those test tubes are more priceless to me than the code to unlimited lives in *Tomb Blaster II*. In the wrong hands

they could make a powerful stink
bomb.
And these look like the wrong
hands.

CHAPTER SEVENTEEN

" . . . **a**nd if it *had* worked," Eraserhead said, pointing to several levers, a handful of cogs, a spring, four spark plugs, a counterweight, two drive belts, and a rotating thing that kept beeping, "this would've pressed this lever here, which would've released this thing, causing this part to shoot way up into the air." He paused and looked up. "*That* would've been cool," Eraserhead concluded, drooping his shoulders.

No one cared. The sound of lone, enthusiastic clapping rose above the silence. Reese, tight in the grip of Eraserhead's big brother, clapped and cheered as if his life depended on it — because it did.

Ms. Miller nervously gripped the stage curtain. "This is going dreadfully. Am I wrong? Please tell me I'm wrong."

Dewey looked up. He smiled at first, then his eyes widened.

"Excuse me," Dewey said.

"What for?" Ms. Miller asked.

Dewey took three large, silent steps backward. Ms. Miller watched him for a moment, then a certain scent hit her nose. I've been at the wrong end of that smell before. Following Dewey's lead, she took three even larger steps backward.

While Dewey gassed Ms. Miller, the Krelboyne kids ate lunch at a picnic table directly behind Mom and "the girls." Dabney picked up his hamburger. At the last moment, he stumbled upon one of the most horrifying discoveries of his life. His hamburger was pink.

"My soyburger . . ." he stammered in terror. "It's bleeding!"

I think the technical term is medium-rare?

Lloyd, now free from the grip of the evil Nixon electromagnet, examined his own hot dog. "Please, please don't let it be," he whimpered, realizing he had already eaten several bites. Lloyd's eyes scanned the *thing* resting between the hot dog bun.

"It's meat!" he shouted in horror. "We're eating meat!"

"Oh, my God!" Dabney screamed and dropped his burger like it was on fire.

One of the cool things about throwing a big rock in the middle of a calm lake is watching the shock waves ripple outward. Let's just say that meat was one big rock. A chain reaction of panic and disgust swept through the Krelboynes. They gagged and screamed. Each one tried to spit out the offending food from their geeky vegetarian bodies.

One Krelboyne dashed past my dad clutching his throat. "Meat! Meat! We've been contaminated by meat!" he shouted.

Dad watched the Krelboyne run into a tree with a dull thud. Dad look around, then untied his cooking apron. He rolled it up and dropped it on the grill. It burst into flames, and he bolted for cover himself.

There was, like, no way he was going to get caught. I know that feeling! Destroying the evidence is *always* the first step.

Dad ran toward the Academic Circus stage, but changed course when he heard the loud boom. The ground shook and a large black cloud erupted from behind the stage curtain.

It was like the end of the world! This gross black cloud blocked out the sun and stunk worse than Dewey.

It would've been so cool — if it wasn't my fault.

Behind the stage curtain, I fell to the ground, a test tube in each hand. I only wanted to make a distraction with Stevie's chemistry set, not a miniature nuclear disaster! Faced with destruction beyond my control, I did what any kid would do: I ran.

I ran for the corner — and smacked right into my dad. We fell to the ground.

"I didn't do it!" we each shouted at the other as the panicked screams of parents, teachers, and children filled the air.

"It's Not My Fault!" [How Did That Sound?]

Okay, there're a few things I learned today. I think the most important one is that the difference between a really cool stink bomb intended to drive away an audience, and a level-three toxic biohazard that's threatening to melt my whole family is apparently two extra drops of sulfur tetraoxide. I'm like totally suing that Web site.

Besides, this isn't my fault. It isn't. I mean, kids shouldn't be able to play with toxic chemicals. And this just proves it. Think about it. I can't go to a movie that has a naked person in it, but I can totally go buy all the ingredients to gas my neighborhood from the comfort of my own home. Who made up that rule? Can't vote. Can't drive. Can't get a credit card. Can go on the Internet and learn to make chemical weapons.

And that's why none of this is my fault. It's society's. I'm merely a victim acting out the pressures of higher learning forced upon younger kids before they're emotionally developed and facing an overwhelming techo-interface that devolves intersocial skills and values. Or something.

Who cares as long as my mom buys it?

CHAPTER EiGHTEEN

The two firefighters arrived in haz-mat suits. They looked like yellow aliens in a big red fire truck. They charged through the stage curtains to the source of the black smoke. They were fast. They were brutal. Stevie's chemical set never had a chance.

You know what stinks? This would've made a cool movie.

Some Krelboynes rolled on the ground. Others rocked silently. The danger had passed, but parents still panicked.

"First the meat and now *this*!" one parent shouted. "I'm writing a letter to the school board!"

And in the middle of it all an angry Stevie wheeled after the firefighter who carried away his chemicals.

"I have . . . a complete . . . inventory of . . . every item," he said, hot on the heels of the ignoring firefighter. "I want . . . a receipt!"

I had two ideas: damage control and a quiet exit. I had ruined the picnic, shattered the circus, and endangered hundreds of lives. That was a small sacrifice for being a free man.

I searched the schoolyard for the rest of my family. I spotted Reese first. He was hanging out with the Eraserheads. Hanging by his underwear to be exact. Eraserhead's big brother held Reese by the elastic band of his "tighty-whities."

"I love Krelboynes. And I swear I'm not just saying that," Reese insisted. "Why would I?"

"Say it with verisimilitude," Eraserhead insisted, pushing his glasses farther up his nose bridge.

"Verisimi-what?" Reese asked. "I thought that was pasta." His voice cracked slightly. Eraserhead's big brother shifted his grip and sent the wedgie higher.

That's *gotta* hurt.

"Nice hang time," Eraserhead said to his big brother.

"It's really a simple function of the elastic waistband's tensile strength," Eraserhead's big brother babbled.

I spotted Francis next. He was still a lost cause, bounding up to Jody who waited for him under a tree.

"Miss me?" Francis asked in the delicate tone of a chirping bird.

"Mm-hmm," Jody responded coldly. She checked the nails on her right hand. She lifted her eyes and shot a look at Francis. "So, who was that girl with her hands all over you?"

Francis looked around. "You mean the paramedic? She was checking to make sure I didn't inhale any toxic fumes."

"And I'm sure you loved *every* minute of it," Jody sneered.

"Would you quit nagging me?" Francis spat.

Jody stood up and moved closer to Francis. "Well, maybe I wouldn't be so jealous if you paid a little more attention to me!" Her voice raised an octave. She sounded like she was going to pop.

"More attention?" Francis waved both arms in the air. "You're smothering me! I need more space."

"Oh, you'll get your space!" She notched her voice up one more octave and the volume to ten. "We're *through!*"

"Fine . . . by . . . me." Francis paused between each word to add more drama.

Jody yanked a ring off her finger. "Here's the school ring you gave me!" she yelled and threw the jewelry at Francis's feet.

Francis reached into his pocket. He pulled out his keys and yanked a trinket off the end. "Your teddy bear key chain," he said coolly and dropped it in Jody's hand.

"Your sweater and the book you lent me," Jody returned, increasing the speed of the schoolyard divorce.

"Your Depeche Mode tape . . ."

"Your school photo . . ."

"Your locket . . ."

"Your letter . . ."

"Your *poems* . . ."

"Your gum." Francis took the pink glob from his mouth. Jody snatched it from his hand and plopped it in her mouth. She spun around and stomped off, chewing all the way.

Francis watched her and let out a small breath.

Or maybe it was a whimper?

After watching Francis and the girl who stopped me from escaping in the first place (maybe this was *her* fault), like all bad criminals, I returned to the scene of the crime.

But instead of finding some crafty detective waiting for me to slip up before nailing me, I came across something much worse.

It was Ms. Miller. Tears poured down her face. White face paint mixed with red, blue, and green ran down her cheeks like a melting rainbow. Her droopy flower and top hat were gone. They were crushed in the panic.

Want to know the only thing worse than a clown? A crying clown. Who's also my teacher. And who's crying because . . . of . . . me.

"I brought you a cheeseburger," I offered, holding out the sandwich I had intended to eat myself. This should make us about even.

"Thank you," Ms. Miller sobbed, taking the food. She bit into the cheeseburger and asked, "Is this meat?"

"Uh . . . it might be." I smacked myself in the head. Ms. Miller was a vegetarian. Can I do anything right today?

Ms. Miller stopped for a moment, then wolfed down the hamburger. "Look what I've been reduced to," she lamented, her mouth full of meat.

I had driven her to carnivorism. The crowning glory in a day of dismal consequences. I slowly backed away.

"Okay, well, I guess —" I couldn't find the right words. Were there right words? What could I say? *I didn't mean to ruin everything and blow up the school and drive you to eat meat.* No. The best I could do was to just say sorry and leave.

"I'm sor —"

"I'm sorry, Malcolm," Ms. Miller interrupted between burger bites.

Huh? *She's* sorry? What was she sorry for? She didn't do anything. Why on earth should she be — *uh-oh.* Trouble.

"I'm sorry," she sniffed. "I know how much you were looking forward to doing your act, especially with your family here, and because of me, you can't. I screwed up everything. I've failed you."

"No, you didn't," I quietly responded, putting my hand on her shoulder.

"Yes, I did," she continued. "And after today, they're going to fire my butt so fast. My parents were right. I should have never left the cannery."

Then the floodgates opened. Noah had to deal with forty days and forty nights on his ark, but my flood was much worse; mine was caused by the tears of a crying woman. And she was crying because of something I did.

"Want another burger?" I asked, my voice wrapped with guilt.

"Yes!" Ms. Miller wailed.

Closer to Free?

I can't believe a day that started out so simple got so totally stupid. That's why it's tough being a kid. You're at the mercy of people older, bigger, and richer than you on a daily basis. If Mom or Dad didn't want to perform in some stupid Academic Circus, they'd just say no. They wouldn't have to sweat out the whole day, hoping for an earthquake or some disaster to save them. They'd just say no.

That's why being an adult is great. At a certain age, society gives you the power of no.

Eat those lima beans!

No.

Baby-sit your brother!

No.

Clean your room!

No.

I can't wait. When you're an adult, you don't have to deal with all the crud

that's pushed on kids. Being an adult
means you're steering your own ship.
No one tells you what to do or when
to do it. You're free to live the life
you choose and you stop doing all
those things you don't want to.
 Don't you?

CHAPTER NiNETEEN

I sat at the picnic table next to my parents, wallowing in self-pity.

"Can you believe it? Meat?" Dad stated, shocked that someone would bring cooked flesh to a vegetarian picnic. "I don't know about you, but I for one am outraged."

The other parents nodded in agreement.

I watched Dorene make her way to a group of parents gathered around Ms. Miller like a pack of hyenas. There were shouts and accusations. Someone yelled "debacle." Another parent threatened to tell Principal Littledove "everything." Watching Ms. Miller in the middle of that pack, it finally hit me. Being an adult doesn't mean you can say no whenever you want to. Kids, parents, grandparents . . . everyone was a prisoner to the same unfairness, so being an adult meant you took the responsibility to say yes?

Wait. Being an adult *sucked*.

I turned to Francis, whose head was also down on the picnic table.

"Can I ask you a question?"

"Yes! All women are the same!" Francis moaned, his face still lying between his arms. "They break your heart and stomp on the pieces."

"No. I mean you'd still like me, even if you found out I was a freak, right? And the family wouldn't be any different, right?"

Francis raised his head. "Dude, we already know you're smart."

"Yeah, but . . ." I let out a long sigh. There was no turning back. Part of me had hoped Francis would've convinced me otherwise and part of me was glad he hadn't. "Just don't say I didn't warn you."

I stood at the table, clenched both fists, and took a deep breath. Before me was the Academic Circus stage. Behind me were toxic hazards, Stevie's chemicals, and Carnivore Caroline the Crying Clown. I looked at my family one last time.

I climbed the stage stairs. My feet were heavier than lead.

"Look!" Lloyd cried out from the crowd. "It's Malcolm."

Like rays of sun breaking through a terrible storm, hope shined down on Ms. Miller the moment she turned and saw me nervously standing on the stage.

"Ooh! Everybody! Quiet! He's doing it! Malcolm's doing it!" she called out. But the crowd continued to argue and mill about. "Shut up!" she screamed.

Amazingly, they did. Once the Krelboyne kids saw me, they eagerly dragged their parents to the audience seats. They stared at me. I stared back.

"I hope he does more than this," my dad whispered to Mom.

I shuffled my feet and scanned my family's faces. This would be the test. Accepting you for who you are is what families are supposed to do? Right?

"Um . . ." I began nervously, "could somebody please hold up a credit card?"

Both Dave and Eraserhead's father complied. I glanced at the cards for a brief second, then closed my eyes.

"Okay, the numbers on them are 3699 7412 6823 9140 and 3424 1804 1835 3668."

Dave and Eraserhead's father looked at their respective cards. "He's right," Dave called out in awe.

A few members of the audience gave light applause. They demanded blood.

"Okay," I sighed. "If you add the individual digits on each card, you get seventy-four and sixty-six. If you multiply those numbers, you get 4,884."

"How do we know he's even right?" Dorene asked disruptively, standing in the middle of the crowd.

"Oh, he's right!" Eraserhead shouted, thrusting out a calculator displaying the same answer.

The audience erupted with applause. I had them. Now it was time to go in for the kill. I covered my eyes and concentrated.

"4,884 squared is 23,853,456." I rattled off numbers faster than an auctioneer. "The square root of 4,884 is 69.885. The square root of *that* is 8.3597."

The crowd was stunned. Did I go too far? Did I go beyond their ability to accept the freakish?

"Factor . . . it!" Stevie shouted out, cracking the stunned silence.

"The factors are two, two, two, and seventy-three," I responded instantly, silently thanking my friend for the ice-breaking save.

"Multiply by pi!" Lloyd called out.

"26.261!"

"Cube it!" shouted Dabney.

"584.214!"

"What's the arc tangent?" yelled Eraserhead.

"89.9 degrees!"

Enthusiasm swept through the crowd. Challenges were called out from every corner and every age group. I let my mind go free. It soared across a vast expanse of numbers, shapes, and theorems. My closed eyes fluttered like I was dreaming. I snapped back answers as instantly as questions were called out.

"Natural log!"

"Reciprocal!"

"Base eight!"

"6.3699! .0017! 11431!" I shouted back with triumphant glee.

"What's the capital of Iceland!" Dabney shouted.

I stopped and opened my eyes. "Reykjavík," I shouted back. "But that's not math."

The crowd burst from their seats and exploded with applause. I was stunned. I didn't know what to do. As quickly as I had ruined the Academic Circus, it was like I rode in on a white charger and saved it.

CHAPTER TWENTY

The dreaded day was finally ending. Reese's underwear band had torn, and he had escaped from Eraserhead's big brother. Francis's heart had taken the first step on its long road to recovery. Dewey hadn't eaten anything too poisonous. Dad had tainted the food supply. Mom was exhausted. We made our way to the car, passing Dorene one last time.

"Why can't you do like that Malcolm?" Dorene tugged on Dabney's ear. "Cellular mitosis? What are we paying your tutor for?"

Mom gave her a finger wave. Dorene released Dabney's ear like a kid whose hand was caught in the cookie jar.

I made my way past Ms. Miller. She was still surrounded by the same pack of parents who had screamed at her minutes ago. Now they patted her back and shook her hand. Ms. Miller and I caught each other's eyes for a moment. I realized the depth of her gratitude for my save.

As my family climbed into the van, Stevie rolled up to say good-bye.

"Was it as bad as I think it was?" I asked.

"Man. You . . . killed," Stevie replied, trying to hide his envy.

"That's what I was afraid of. Sorry you didn't get to do your act," I said earnestly.

"Can . . . the sympathy . . . showboat."

That last word made me flinch.

Now came the real test. The freaky Krelboyne audience had loved me, but what about my family?

Hesitantly, I climbed into the back of the van. A car full of astonished stares met me. Is this what I get for being nice? Now my own family is scared of me?

The uncomfortable silence stretched like taffy. Then Dewey tugged on Dad's shirt. "Is Malcolm a robot?" he asked.

"No, son," Dad answered. "He's just smart." He started the van and adjusted the rearview mirror. "Very, very, very, very, very, very smart."

I could have handled four "verys," maybe even five. But six? No one should be expected to handle six "verys" in a row. I felt tears well in my eyes. I knew the moment anybody saw me cry, Dewey would ask, "Won't Malcolm rust?"

I tried to blink them back. I tried to remember how happy Ms. Miller was and how I had saved her job. I had done the right thing. Right? Maybe in ten or fifteen years, my family wouldn't be afraid of me anymore? I hung my head. No one would see the tears. No one.

"Hey, Malcolm . . . ?"

It was Francis. Great. What's he going to ask, if I run on unleaded or regular gas?

"Malcolm?"

"Yeah," I responded, without looking.

"How many fingers am I holding up?" Francis quipped.

I slowly looked up to see Francis was only holding up one finger . . . the middle one. A smile cracked across my sad face. "Shut up," I said in a low voice.

"Hey, Malcolm! Hey!" Reese said excitedly. "Analyze what I had for lunch." Reese leaned hard against me and let out a huge burp in my face.

"Get off me, you moron!" I laughed. "You are so gross!"

"Not as gross as your face!" Reese prodded back.

"I don't understand it," Mom said from the front seat. "You can rattle off a bunch of numbers, but you can't even remember to brush your teeth?"

I laughed harder than I had ever done in my life. It was a laugh of joy. My fears drained from my body and sunk into the floor. I was wrong. It didn't matter how freaky my family thinks I am, they love me. I'll always be *their* freak.

"All right," Dad called out. "Who's ready for Burger Barn?"

Finally, I could relax. Nothing had changed. My family was exactly as they had been this morning and every other morning of my entire life.

Wait. Is that a *good* thing?

Wasted Wishes? Nah.

I used to be Malcolm. Just plain and simple Malcolm. Now I'm a Krelboyne. It's weird, though, finding out that I'm a genius.

My mom says people like me owe the rest of the world something. But I don't think that's fair. It's not like I asked to be super-intelligent. If I could ask for anything, it'd be new video games, unlimited movie rentals, or pizza for dinner every night. Who gets wishes and wastes them on "I'd like to be smarter, please?"

But I'm not going to let it bother me. I'm just a kid, right? Things can only get better!

Can you tell me again just when that's supposed to happen?

A whole day at a water park — wave pools and log flume rides and junk food! How cool is that? For most kids, it would be amazing.

But most kids don't have Reese, aka "he lives to make my life miserable" alongl Who spends the whole time humiliating and punching and shoving you. And most kids have parents who actually might stop what they're doing to try and stop Reese from doing what he's doing.

And, then on the way home, most kids don't have the bad luck to get stuck in the biggest, worst, ultimate traffic jam of all time. On the hottest day of all time. With a dad who reacts by wandering around wondering about the meaning of life. And a mom who gets up in a forklift . . . oh, never mind. You get the picture.

Most kids aren't Malcolm.

Incoming: Here's a sneak preview of what happened to him that day. You can read the rest of it by picking up the book called *Malcolm in the Middle: Water Park.* (But no reading until an hour after you get of the pool.)

WATER PARK

CHAPTER ONE

Twenty-four hours to go and we're outta here! Mom and Dad are taking us to Wavetown USA — the big water park. It's just water, slides, and no Krelboynes.

I'm ready to go, like, *now*, but my dad needs a day of preparation.

Mom slid the clippers along his hairy back with the skill of a race car driver. She clicked off the buzzing shears and admired her work.

"There you go, Hal," she said proudly. "All pink and shiny."

"Boys!" Dad called out.

Reese and I picked up two mirrors from the table. We held them behind Dad.

"I feel ten pounds lighter," Dad said, admiring his creamy-smooth and hairless back.

Some families have movie night or game night as bonding traditions. My family has "shave Dad's back." Usually, I don't look forward to it. I mean, who would? Right? I'm totally picking Dad hair off me for the next three days.

But for a trip to Wavetown USA? It's worth every hair-picking minute.

Dad braced himself against the table. Next came the one thing I've never understood about shaving: the aftershave lotion.

Mom poured a full bottle of it onto a washcloth and smacked it onto my dad's back.

"Hoo-hoo-hoo. That stings! Ha-ha-ha," Dad exhaled as the cloth was peeled away.

"Smooth as a seal," Dad enthused, a tone of pain lingering in his voice. "I'm ready for that water-slide."

Back in the '70s, my dad was one of the coolest kids in school. Too bad that was, like, forever ago. He's still stuck in that ancient time when bands had stupid names like "Foghat."

"We haven't had an outing in quite a while," Mom added as she tossed the empty aftershave bottle in the trash. "It's nice when we can do things together as a family."

Wait a second. Was this *my* family? Everyone is happy. Everything is going well. Everything is —

Dewey. I *knew* this was too easy.

Dewey's like a tiny wind up toy whose switch is stuck on high gear. He never sits still, not even when he's asleep. If he's not flopping around, rolling around, or kicking, he's thinking about flopping around, rolling around, or kicking.

INTRODUCING THE NEW
Malcolm in the Middle
BOOK SERIES, BASED ON THE HIT TV SHOW!

MALCOLM IN THE MIDDLE #1: LIFE IS UNFAIR

MALCOLM IN THE MIDDLE #2: WATER PARK

MALCOLM IN THE MIDDLE: MY CLASS PROJECT

AVAILABLE NOW AT A BOOKSTORE NEAR YOU!
www.scholastic.com

SCHOLASTIC

MAL1000